Adapted by Beth Beechwood

Based on the series created by Michael Poryes and Rich Correll & Barry O'Brien

Part One is based on the episode, "Good Golly, Miss Dolly," Written by Sally Lapiduss

Part Two is based on the episode, "Mascot Love," Written by Sally Lapiduss

DISNEY
CHANNEL

DISNEY
PRESS

New York

Printed in the United States of America

Second Edition
9 10

Library of Congress Catalog Card Number: 2006937639
ISBN-13: 978-14231-0461-2
ISBN-10: 1-4231-0461-7

For more Disney Press fun, visit www.disneybooks.com
Visit DisneyChannel.com

PART ONE

Chapter One

It was a regular day at Seaview Middle School—regular, except for the fact that Principal Fisher was retiring. All the students were busy creating farewell videos to pay tribute to him, and Oliver Oken was in charge of taping. He was wielding his camera all over school, driving everyone crazy. At the moment, his focus was on Lilly Truscott, who wasn't exactly eloquent in these types of situations.

"We're going to miss you, Principal

Fisher," Lilly said. "I can't believe you're retiring. You don't look a day over eighty." Lilly thought this was the perfect thing to say.

Oliver leaned around his camera. "Lilly, he's only sixty-five!"

"Really?" Lilly said dramatically, her face dropping. "Is he sick?" She was *sure* he was older.

"He will be after he sees this," Oliver joked, swinging the camera over to Danny for an interview. Oliver narrated: "Let's see what farewell words Dandruff Danny has for Principal Fisher."

Danny scratched his head. "One second," he muttered, "let me fix my hair." Then a snowfall of dandruff cascaded off his head. This wasn't going to be Oscar material.

"This is gonna take a while," Oliver

noted. Right on cue, Lilly's head popped back into the camera's viewfinder. She apparently felt the need to redeem herself.

"I was just kidding before, sir," she said into the camera. "It's not that you're *old*, it's just that you remind me of my dead grand-father. But he didn't die of old age—he got hit by a school bus." She smiled at that. "Ironic, isn't it?" She just couldn't stop talking. With every word, she made it a lit-tle worse. Oliver swung the camera around, searching for his next victim, but he landed instead on the man himself, Principal Fisher. Oliver's surprise shook the camera.

"Principal Fisher!" he exclaimed as he put down his camera.

"Now, Oken," Principal Fisher said, feigning embarrassment. "I hope this isn't some video farewell to a beloved retiring principal." He had barely finished speaking when a wad of paper struck him right in the head. Maybe "beloved" wasn't quite the word. "Hey," he yelled in the direction of the tossed paper. "All right, you girls, hold it right there!" And he was gone.

"I want to do mine over again," Lilly pleaded to Oliver.

"We'll clean it up in editing," he said dismissively, suddenly noticing his friend Miley Stewart. She was leaning against a wall, staring into space, and chewing gum as if it were her job. She looked nervous. Oliver approached her. "Miley?" he asked. Nothing. He tried again. "Miley?"

But Miley paid him no mind. She was in another universe entirely. Oblivious to her friends, she took a deep breath and walked right past them . . . and right toward Jake Ryan. Jake, the star of a hit TV show, was a teen heartthrob. But his fame wasn't a secret the way Miley's was. All the girls loved him and fawned all over him. Miley did, too, but only in her mind. To his face, she tried to be the cool, collected girl who treated him like a regular guy. After all, she kind of understood how it could be—that's why she kept her "other" life a secret. At that moment, Jake was chatting up two other girls, Amber and Ashley, and Miley just wouldn't have it. In her fantasy, she pushed the girls out of the way. "Move over, girls," she said, not even looking at them. Her eyes were fixed on Jake. She grabbed him by the collar. "Listen, Jake, and listen good. There's only one dame in the world that's right for a guy like you, and you're looking at her."

Jake didn't miss a beat. Talking tough in return, he asked, "What took you so long, baby?"

"Traffic," Miley said quickly. "Now plant one on me and make me remember why I waste my time with you."

They moved in for a kiss when Miley's daydream was interrupted by an annoying buzzing sound.

"Miley? Miley?" It wasn't really buzzing. It was just Oliver.

Miley finally snapped out of it, her lips still puckered. "What?" she asked, confused. Why was he being so annoying? So it took her a minute to answer. Jeez.

"You were dreaming about Jake, weren't you?" Lilly asked in her usual, right-down-to-business kind of way. Miley continued to be defensive.

"No, I wasn't. Why would I do that? I am so over him," she stated firmly. But Jake walked right by them at that very moment.

"Hey, Miley," he said, nodding in her direction.

"I'm over you, okay? Move on with your life!" She shouted and stormed off in a huff.

Jake shrugged. "I was just gonna tell her that her shoe's untied." As soon as the words were out of Jake's mouth, Miley tripped on her shoelace. "Whoa!" she yelled as she fell down. This was not good. Her crush was starting to cause her physical pain. She got through the rest of the day, although she was a little distracted by her feelings for Jake. Luckily, she had a recording session scheduled for that afternoon. That would help.

When Miley got to the studio, she changed into her Hannah gear to get herself out of the part of regular schoolgirl with a schoolgirl crush and into the part of *teen pop star* with a schoolgirl crush. She was recording her new song, and she was determined to get it right. For hours, Mr. Stewart and an engineer watched and listened closely. But as Miley was doing one last take, her voice drifted off. "I can't sing this anymore. I mean, it's not like girls just stand around dreaming about boys all day," she protested.

Mr. Stewart pressed a button that enabled him to talk to Miley through the glass. "You okay, darlin'?" He was a little concerned. His daughter just didn't seem like herself lately, and he wondered what was going on.

"Of course. I'm fine. It's just that there are other more important things in life, like world peace and . . . whales," she lamented. "Why can't we do a song about whales? And not stupid boy whales. Girl whales. Happy, independent girl whales."

"I'll get right on that, darlin'. 'Girl whales, doin' their nails, don't need no males'— practically writes itself," he joked.

"Daddy, I'm not saying that's exactly the song. I'm open to other fish, too. Can I take a break?" This was going nowhere. She took off her headphones and walked out of the booth. She needed some time alone to daydream about Jake in peace.

"I think that's a good idea. Besides, there's somebody here who wants to see ya," Mr. Stewart said.

"Oh, Dad, I'm not in the mood to see anybody right now," Miley said as her surprise guest walked in.

"Well, fine. You don't want to see me, I'll just turn the bus around and head on back to Nashville," said the guest, Miley's Aunt

Dolly. Well, she wasn't *exactly* Miley's aunt—more like a "god-aunt," but that was just fine with Miley.

Aunt Dolly was the kindest, funniest person Miley knew. She was a little quirky, with a country metaphor for just about everything, but her charm was infectious. Miley adored her.

"Aunt Dolly!" Miley was so excited. She ran over to give her a big hug.

Dolly held Miley at arm's length to get a better look at her. "Look at you," she exclaimed. "You're sproutin' like a rose-bush after a month of rain, only not as wet and twice as pretty." That was the kind of Dolly-ism Miley loved.

Apparently, Robby liked that one, too. "Ooh, doggies, I like that," Miley's dad yelped. "Might use it in a song."

"Well, that's fine," Dolly replied. "First

one's free, next one I'm taking half the profits with me." They all laughed. Then Dolly linked arms with Miley and led her in the direction of the recording booth. "Now come in here, I got a story to tell ya about this possum and skunk that were sharing a 'pe-ew' at church—" She closed the door. It seemed the possum story was a ruse. "Okay, what's his name?" she asked.

"What are you talking about?" Miley acted innocent. She had no idea how Aunt Dolly could have found out about Jake. She thought she was being so good about keeping that to herself.

"I'm talking about my goddaughter crushing over some boy harder than a monster truck driving over a little clown car," Aunt Dolly said.

Laughing much harder than necessary, Miley said, "Monster trucks, clown cars, whoooo, I've missed you, Aunt Dolly." She finally stopped laughing and tried to change the subject. She put her arm around her aunt, hoping to make Aunt Dolly forget what they were talking about. "You know, we're thinking about getting a dog."

Aunt Dolly wasn't having any of this. "Well, you might want to name him Zippy, 'cause zip is what I'm getting from you. Listen, sweet pea, when you decide you want to talk about this boy who don't exist, you know I'm here."

"I'm here, too, bud." This was Mr. Stewart's voice from the control booth. He had been listening the whole time.

"Robby Ray, you nosy hillbilly!" Dolly hooted.

"I'm not listening, I just wanted you to know I'm here. And I'm not a nosy hillbilly, I'm a concerned hillbilly father."

Chapter Two

The next morning, country music bounced off the walls of the Stewart household. Aunt Dolly bopped around the kitchen, fixing the flowers she had placed in a vase on the kitchen table right next to the big basket of freshly baked muffins. She had been busy all morning trying to make the house feel more like a home. Mr. Stewart jumped down the stairs in his jogging clothes and took in the scene.

"Mornin', Dolly, I—whoa—" It wasn't just the flowers and muffins in the kitchen—there were pink pillows on the couch and the chairs, and there were flowers everywhere. She had even put out potpourri. "Looks like my home's been invaded by aliens from the Planet Froufrou."

"Robby Stewart, you keep making fun of my decorating and I'm gonna have to tell your kids how you used to run around in a diaper and a pair of black boots sayin' 'Herro, I'm Johnny Cash.'" Aunt Dolly had put on her deepest voice.

Mr. Stewart quickly reconsidered. He sure didn't want his kids to know about that one. "Come to think of it, I love what you've done with it." With that, Aunt Dolly walked over to the stereo, turned it off, and picked up the video camera that was sitting right there. She turned the camera toward Mr. Stewart.

"Could you say that to the folks back home? And while you're at it, would you please tell your Uncle Zeke to get rid of that awful mullet comb-over. Lord knows how he can take one hair and wrap it completely around his head and down his back."

"It's called a skullet, and it ain't that bad," Mr. Stewart offered.

"Well, you ain't seen him floss with it."

Mr. Stewart looked into the camera. "Hey, everybody. Hey, Uncle Zeke, you might want to treat yourself to a haircut and get you a toothpick. I'm going for a jog." Just as his dad headed out the back door, Jackson, Miley's brother, came down the stairs, sniffing his own shirt. "Oh, man. This is not good," he said out loud.

"Oh, what's the matter with you?" Aunt Dolly asked with tremendous compassion.

"Aunt Dolly, I smell like a petunia. What did you wash this stuff in?"

"A little fabric softener and a whole lotta love," she giggled as she turned the camera on him. "Got anything to say to the folks back home?"

"Well, sure," he said with a coy smile. "Hey, everybody, when the guys get a whiff of me, I'm gonna get beat up today! Bye," he said with exaggerated enthusiasm and a big thumbs-up.

As soon as he was out the front door, Dolly turned the camera on herself. "Well, at least you got a look at him before that happens. Now, let's go check on Miley and see what she's up to." Dolly headed out to the deck where she found Miley playing her guitar and singing. Dolly paused to take it in.

"Well, that was just beautiful, sweet

pea," Aunt Dolly said to Miley when she finished her song. "I can't wait to hear you sing it when there really is a boy."

Miley thought about that for a minute and decided to take a leap of faith and open up to her Aunt Dolly. What could it hurt, really? She put down her guitar and looked at Dolly. "His name is Jake . . . Jake Ryan."

Dolly gasped, indicating to Miley that she knew who Jake was. "The Zombie Slayer?!" She hopped into Jake's zombie-slaying stance. "'Dude, I slayed you once, don't make me slay you again'," she said, quoting Jake. "That boy is too cuuuuute!"

"I know, he goes to my school. And sometimes he can be really obnoxious, but then he gets really sweet, but then he gets all obnoxious again," Miley was aware that she was a rambling a little but she didn't care.

"That reminds me, I gotta call my husband," Dolly was always the comedian.

"Aunt Dolly!" Miley insisted, pointing her finger toward herself dramatically, "Puberty crisis here!" Miley got up and grabbed her guitar. She headed into the house, followed by Aunt Dolly, who was holding her video camera.

"Darlin', I am so sorry," she pleaded. "I just forget sometimes. Being a teenage girl is harder than walking through a balloon shop with a porcupine purse."

Miley plopped herself down on the couch. "I don't know what to do, Aunt Dolly. Jake said he liked me 'cause I'm the only girl at school who's not falling all over him. If I tell him I like him, then I *am* falling all over him. . . ." She paused and made a face at her aunt. "I'm caught between a rock and a Zombie Slayer here!"

Dolly placed the camera on the coffee table and sat down next to Miley. "Well, honey, nobody knows what's around the corner. But I know one thing—if you keep yourself out of the game for fear of losin', there is no way on this earth you're ever gonna win."

"So, you're saying I should just walk up to Jake and say, 'Jake Ryan, I'm through pretending I don't like you, when the truth is . . . I'm totally in love with you.'?" Just then, something caught Miley's eye. It was the red light on the video camera. "Wait a minute," she said, closing in on the camera. "Is this thing on?"

Dolly hurried to pick up the camera and quickly switch it off. "Oh, good golly, Miss Dolly, I am forever leaving this thing on. Last Christmas, I got four hours of the dog chewing the head off the Little Drummer

Boy. Poor little old Rufus was chuckin' up body parts for a week." Right on cue, Dolly's cell phone rang. Miley couldn't exactly tell where the ringing was coming from, though—could it be . . . ?

"Uh, Aunt Dolly, I think your hair's ringing," Miley said. Dolly put the camera back on the table, then she reached into her hair and pulled out a cell phone. She noticed Miley's surprise at this revelation.

"Well, honey, when your pants are as tight as mine, you have to have somewhere to put your phone." She picked up the phone and talked into it. "Hey, sweetie, I was just talking about you. Rufus ate what? No." Then she whispered to Miley, "I'll be right back," before turning her attention back to the person on the phone. "He did? The one on the patio?" Dolly needed some privacy to discuss her dog's digestive problems, so she went out onto the deck. The moment she was gone, Lilly and Oliver barged through the front door, and Miley had company again. Oliver, like Aunt Dolly, had his video camera with him.

"Miles," Oliver said. "I gotta get this video in today and you're the only one who hasn't said good-bye to Principal Fisher. So take your time, think of something really good. And . . . action!" He hadn't given her any time at all, of course.

Miley looked straight into the camera's lens and said flatly, "Bye."

"Perfect!" Oliver said before becoming distracted by something else. "Ooh, muffins." He put his camera down on the coffee table next to Aunt Dolly's and made a beeline for the muffins on the kitchen table.

Meanwhile, Lilly was still mad at herself

over her little faux pas. "'Bye,'" she imitated Miley. "Why didn't I do that? 'A day over eighty,'" she said, quoting herself in disgust. "What was I thinking?" A car honked from outside, stopping Lilly from being any harder on herself.

"Oh, that's Mom," Oliver informed them. "I have to get to school early so I can turn this thing in to the editor." They heard Oliver's mom shout from outside.

"Oliver, let's go!" It was a deeper voice than expected. Oliver grabbed the camera off the table and rushed to the door.

"I thought you said that was your mom," Lilly said.

"It is," Oliver replied. "When she's mad, she uses her man voice." He ran outside, and Lilly and Miley heard the deep voice say, "Move, move, move!"

Lilly noticed a camera still on the table.

"Wait a minute, I thought he took his camera."

"Oh, that's Aunt Dolly's," Miley assured her.

"Funny. It looks a lot like Oliver's," Lilly said skeptically.

"Yeah, but Aunt Dolly's has her initial on it. See?" Miley picked up the camera and turned it on its side, expecting to show Lilly the letter *D* Dolly had stuck on it. Miley's face quickly turned pale. "Where's the *D*?" She turned the camera every which way. "Where's the rhinestone *D*?" she asked frantically.

"Miley. It's just a camera. What's the big deal?" Lilly had no idea what they were dealing with here. This was not good.

"That camera has a tape in it of me saying, 'Jake, I'm totally in love with you!'" Miley shouted.

"Whoa!" was all Lilly could say in return.

"I know."

What were they going to do now? They both dashed out the door and headed back to school. They had to get ahold of Oliver.

Chapter Three

Miley and Lilly were out of breath. They had run all the way to school and now found themselves in the hallway, facing Jake. He was at his locker, wearing a very cool pair of jeans and a gorgeous blazer. They slowed way down and tried to act cool.

"Hey, Jake," Miley offered casually.

"'Sup?" Lilly followed.

Jake merely nodded at the girls as they

passed by. Once they were out of his line of vision, they resumed their race to Oliver's locker.

"Quick, Oliver, you took the wrong camera! Give it back," Miley demanded of her friend.

"Oh, sorry. Here," Oliver said. Miley handed Oliver his camera and grabbed Aunt Dolly's camera out of his hand. She opened the tape compartment as quickly as she could. It was empty.

"Where's the tape?" she asked. She was freaking out at the thought of where it might be and where it might end up!

"I gave it to the editor." Oliver was being so nonchalant. He clearly did not understand the implications of this.

"Who's the editor?" Lilly interrogated.

They watched in horror as Oliver pointed in the direction of Jake. "Jake," he said.

Miley grabbed Oliver's collar and growled at him. "Jake . . . who?!"

"Ow, ow, thanks a lot." Oliver winced. "You ripped out my only chest hair." Miley let him go at that, looking positively distraught. "So I gave Jake the tape," Oliver continued. "Just go ask for it back."

As if it would be so easy, she thought, turning to Lilly with a pained face. "I can't believe I have to do this." She took a deep breath and made a move toward Jake. He was busy talking with Amber and Ashley, or rather, Amber and Ashley were talking to each other with Jake as a witness.

"Jake, can we have our tape back?" Ashley pleaded in a little girl voice.

"Please," Amber joined in. "I looked great but she looked terrible."

Ashley was offended. "Better than you!" she shouted at Amber.

"Keep dreaming!" Amber yelled back. They got in each other's faces, and Miley took this pause as the perfect moment to interrupt. As entertaining as this was, Miley had come on business.

"Uh, Jake?" she asked.

"One second," he said to Miley, before turning to Amber and Ashley. "Guys, if I let you redo your tape then everyone's gonna want to do the same thing. I'm sorry, but nobody gets their tapes back under any circumstances." He turned back to Miley then. "So, Miley, what's going on?" He was always so nice to her. He definitely spoke to her differently than to everyone else. Didn't he?

She had to think fast. There was no way she could ask for it back now. "Uh, I just want to say . . . I know another guy named Jake Ryan. So if you ever hear me talking about a Jake Ryan, it's not *you*, Jake Ryan, it's the *other* Jake Ryan . . . not you, Jake. Other Jake. Bye-bye." She walked away knowing she hadn't accomplished anything, except maybe making herself look like an idiot. As she walked past Oliver, she gave him a squinty, disgusted look. "You're dead to me," she said in a raspy, dramatic voice.

Chapter Four

Back at the Stewart residence, Dolly was wreaking havoc on the guys' masculinity. Jackson bounded down the stairs to find his father with his head in the refrigerator. Jackson's hair was so fluffed up, it looked like he was wearing a wig. "Dad, I don't know why, but I have this funny feeling that Aunt Dolly replaced my shampoo." As his father appeared from behind the refrigerator door, it looked like he understood where Jackson was coming from. Mr. Stewart's hair was equally frizzed out. They both looked a little more like Dolly than they would have liked. Jackson jumped back in surprise.

"Join the club, son. Looks like we've been volumized and Dolly-sized."

"I can't take this anymore, Dad. Between the shampoo, and the smelly tissues, and the potpourri, and all these flowers — I'm losing my manly essence!"

"There's only one thing we can do, son. Let's go to the gym and fight back with the only thing she can't take from us — our man stink."

Jackson took a second to think about this but turned his father down. "Dad, can we do it tomorrow? Aunt Dolly buffed my nails and I don't wanna ruin them."

"Do you hear yourself, son?" Mr. Stewart muttered.

Realizing what he had just said, he looked horrified. "Oh, no, get me to the gym—fast!" The two of them rushed out the front door.

Upstairs, Miley paced back and forth outside her closet, as Lilly, wearing her baseball cap sideways, as usual, tried on every pair of shoes her friend owned. Well, every pair Hannah owned. Miley's shoes were boring.

"I've got to figure out something, Lilly. Jake's probably laughing at that tape right now."

"I know. This is awful, this is horrible, this is . . ." she turned her attention to a cute bag in Miley's closet, " . . . so cute! Can I borrow it?" Lilly was forever distracted by Miley's Hannah wardrobe. Before

Miley could answer, Dolly popped her head into the room. She was carrying a fistful of shopping bags and looking excited.

"Lilly," she said, "put that away. I've got something else for you girls to wear."

"Thanks, Aunt Dolly, but clothes aren't going to help me now." Miley was so blinded by her embarrassment, she couldn't even see that Dolly seemed to have a plan in mind.

Dolly started unloading her bags. "These will." She smirked as she pulled out black clothes and gloves. There was mischief in her giggle. "I got you girls into this mess, and I'm gonna get you out. If that boy won't give the tape back, we'll just go in after it." She looked at the clothes in her hands. "Undercover," she said ominously.

Lilly was psyched. "Ooh, I like the way she thinks!" she said joyfully.

As Miley pulled out a pair of great-looking black boots, she couldn't help but agree. "And I *love* the way she accessorizes!"

"These boots are made for sneaking," Dolly said playfully.

Later that day, the girls and their Mission: Impossible had begun. They were right down the hall from the video-editing room at school. It was very dark, and no one was around. Miley, dressed in her fashionable black commando outfit, moved down the hallway like one of Charlie's Angels. She did a tuck-and-roll and hid behind a plant. Lilly, looking equally stylish, followed Miley's move with a similar one. But Dolly put them both to shame. Out of nowhere, she appeared. Miley winked at her, a cue to begin her entrance, and Dolly did an

Olympics-worthy series of acrobatics—not to mention some break dancing! Miley and Lilly were in awe.

"Wow," said Miley.

"Whoa," echoed Lilly.

Dolly glanced at them and said in a whisper, "Girls, I don't just rock—I roll."

Miley shook off her aunt's skills and said, "Okay, let's just focus on the plan. Aunt Dolly and I go into the edit room. Lilly, you stand watch. We grab the tape and we're outta here." But there was a little glitch in the plan Miley had outlined. They had to get though the main hallway doors first.

Lilly shook the doorknob. "It's locked!" she gasped.

But, just like she had with this whole plan, Dolly was about to come to the rescue once again. "Not for long," she said. "These nails aren't just for scratching." She licked her pinky fingernail and slipped it into the lock. She had it picked within seconds. "Like a charm. I haven't carried a house key in years." She was mighty pleased with herself.

Miley was getting excited now that things were looking up. "Okay, people, let's git'r'done!"

As they continued down the hall toward the editing room, Miley was getting annoyed with the sounds Lilly's shoes were making. With every step, they squeaked. It wasn't exactly helping them stay undercover. She stopped in her tracks and looked at her friend. "Lilly, less squeaky, more sneaky."

"Sorry." Lilly stopped, but the squeaking did not. "Not good," she said.

Finally, they arrived at the editing room door. They all popped their heads up to peek through the glass. "Oh, no. He's in there," Miley said, not sure what to do next.

"What do we do?" asked a frantic Lilly.

They had to think fast. Together, they came up with a new plan. Dolly was the only one Jake didn't know, so she would have to play the biggest role. She ducked into the janitor's closet and found overalls and a cap. Out she came, pushing a cart with a trash can along with some mops and brooms. She would have to go into the room and clean it up. It was their only chance to get the tape back. They all got into position and hoped for the best.

Inside the editing room, Jake was sitting at the editing bay with a stack of tapes next to him. Miley could only hope and pray that he hadn't gotten to theirs yet. In front of him were the messy remnants of a fast-food meal he had eaten. Behind him was the doorway and window below which the three musketeers hid. They snuck a peek at what Jake was doing, then they sent Dolly in.

She shuffled in with her trash can. "Oh, I'm sorry, honey. Mind if I clean up in here? Not that it matters 'cause I'm gonna clean up anyway, so don't you sass me, boy." She wasn't sure where she was going with this and neither was Jake. He looked confused. He wasn't the type of person to sass anyone.

"No problem," he muttered, turning back to his editing equipment. At that moment, Miley popped her head out of the trash can, but Jake started to turn around. Dolly quickly pushed Miley's head back into the can. This was part two of the plan: Miley was hiding in the trash can! "Oh, one sec . . ." he said, calling to Dolly-the-janitor. He gathered the remains of his very messy, ketchup-soaked burger and fries to dump them in her Dumpster. "Might as well toss this," he shrugged.

Miley stuck a hand out and poked Dolly hard. But Dolly understood what she had to do to protect Miley's head from the onslaught of Jake's greasy fast-food remains. "Wait a minute," she said to Jake. "Don't you wanna finish that? You're a growing boy."

"Nah. I eat too much of this junk any-way." He moved to toss the pile in the trash can when Dolly planted herself firmly in front of him.

"Can't let you do that. Union rules. I'll take care of it." Good one, thought Miley. Meanwhile, Dolly took the greasy, goopy wrappers from Jake and just held on to them, not really sure what to do next. "I'll just . . . toss it into the *left* of the trash can." She was doing her best to warn Miley of what was coming. Miley couldn't quite escape the trash completely, and as she tried to rid herself of the mess, her elbows banged into the sides of the can and shook it.

"Whoa, what the heck is in there?" Jake asked.

Dolly didn't miss a beat. "I guess that dead lab frog still has a little hop left in 'im." She looked down at the imaginary frog. "Sorry."

Jake seemed to want to move on from this little chat with the janitor. He took a step toward the tapes piled on the desk.

"Sweet niblets, you're Jake Ryan! You are, aren't you?" Aunt Dolly said, turning Jake around so his back was to the trash can. Miley had work to do.

"Yes," Jake said cautiously. Dolly took this opportunity to escort Jake away from the trash can so that Miley could snag the tape. "Dang, you're as cute as they say you are. Can I have your autograph?" As she said this, Miley popped out of the trash can and grabbed all the tapes with both arms. Then, she disappeared back inside as fast as she could.

Jake didn't seem to notice. "Sure," he replied to Dolly's autograph request. As he signed, Dolly bought some extra time.

"It's for my goddaughter. I mean she just loves you. Really . . . she loves you." Miley rattled the trash can in protest. "That's that dang frog again," Dolly covered.

Suddenly, Jake took notice of his now-empty worktable. "Hey, what happened to all my tapes?" he asked.

"Ribbit, ribbit, gottit." Miley did her

very best to sound like a frog and prayed that she didn't blow it. Then, she tossed a handful of tapes out of the cart. She hoped Jake would suspend his disbelief that a frog could be so . . . strong.

Dolly tried to distract him by talking about his work. "Hey, did you say that very line in the famous 'lost zombie' episode?"

"Yeah. Some of my finest work," he said.

"Well, gotta go," Aunt Dolly said.

"Oh, and one more thing," Jake shouted before tossing his milk shake in the direction of the trash can . . . and Miley.

"Shake in the hole!" Dolly cried, in an attempt to warn Miley.

Then Dolly wheeled the Dumpster and Miley to safety. Lilly closed the door to the editing room and came over to get the news. "Did you get it?" she asked eagerly. Miley stood up, covered in fast food and milk shake mess. But she was victorious. She held up the tape.

"Oh, I got it," she said. "I got it good."

Lilly took a finger to Miley's face and swiped some milk shake for a taste. "Strawberry," Lilly stated.

"Oh, my favorite," Dolly offered cheerfully.

Chapter Five

That evening at the Stewart household, Jackson and his father had come back from their "regain your manliness" workout and were sitting on the couch in the living room, feeling proud of themselves. Hands behind their heads, sweat covering their foreheads, they reflected. "Breathe that in, son," Mr. Stewart instructed Jackson. "That's the sweet stench of independence, freedom, and manly pride."

"I hear ya, Daddy," agreed Jackson.

They sat there for a while, seemingly enjoying their sweaty manhood. Then, Jackson broke the silence with a sniff. "My eyes are burning . . . my eyes," he said dramatically.

Mr. Stewart caught on. "I'm so ranky I can taste my own stanky."

Jackson leaped out of his seat. "I can't stand it. I'm taking a shower . . ." Then he turned serious. ". . . and I'm using Aunt Dolly's peach body wash with exfoliating loofah glove."

"Loofah all you wanna, I'm gonna take a bubble bath with one of her citrus fizzy balls," Mr. Stewart admitted proudly. He sniffed himself and said, "Maybe two." They both headed upstairs.

The next day at school, things were not

quite as cheerful. Miley was at her locker having a bit of a fit. She grabbed her books angrily and slammed her locker shut.

Lilly caught all of this as she approached. "What are you so upset about? You got the tape back," she said.

"I know. I should be happy, but I'm not."

"Well, it makes sense." Lilly said. Then she continued with her theory on Miley's dissatisfaction. "I mean, you're right back where you started, secretly crushing on Jake. If I were you, I would've listened to your Aunt Dolly and just told him how you feel."

"Why didn't you say that yesterday?" Miley was frustrated.

"'Cause I wanted to wear the cool black outfit," she said coyly.

Miley was about to comment on Lilly's motivation when she noticed that Jake was on his way over to his locker. She knew what she had to do. "Okay, I'm gonna do it. I'm gonna tell him the truth. Maybe he'll think I'm falling all over him, but at least he'll know how I feel."

"And maybe he'll feel the same way," Lilly suggested.

"Yeah, you're right," Miley tried to sound optimistic. "It's worth the risk. I'll never know until I try." She walked toward Jake with determination in her steps. "Hey, Jake," she said when she reached his locker.

"Hey, Miley," he said back.

"Look, I've got something to tell you and—" She started to say it but was rudely interrupted by a girl who came up to Jake, kissed him on the cheek, and put her arm through his.

"Hi, Jakey," the girl said sweetly.

"Hey, Rach," Jake said affectionately. Apparently, he knew this girl. "Miley, you know Rachel, right, from Spanish class?"

Miley was positively stunned. "Oh, sure . . . Hi, Rachel."

Then he said it. "Yeah, we're kinda going out now."

"Isn't that great?" Rachel beamed.

"Yeah . . . really great," Miley said flatly.

"So, what was it you wanted to tell me?" Jake asked Miley.

"Nothing. It's not important anymore," Miley said, trying to cover her devastation.

"Okay, well, see ya around," Jake said. He seemed a little concerned for Miley.

"Yeah, see ya around," Miley said sadly. She watched as Jake and Rachel walked away arm in arm, leaving Miley standing there in their wake.

❊ ❊ ❊

Miley made her way home somehow and plopped herself down on the same couch where her dad and Jackson had been sweating earlier. She held one of Aunt Dolly's flowers and was plucking petals from it, having a pity party for herself. "He loves me not . . ." She plucked. "Still not loving me . . ." She plucked. "Too busy loving Rachel . . . He still ain't loving me, and he ain't gonna love me. I need more petals . . ." There were petals everywhere — the couch and the coffee table were barely visible anymore.

Mr. Stewart and Aunt Dolly looked on at this sad scene from the kitchen. "You got any ideas what we're gonna do about this?" Miley's father asked.

Aunt Dolly looked disappointed in him. "Have you ever known me not to have an idea?" she asked. "Just follow my lead."

She headed into the living room with Mr. Stewart right behind her.

"So, Robby, do you remember when you were trying to get up the courage to ask Miley's mom out and she just turned you down flat?" Aunt Dolly asked Mr. Stewart loudly.

"Yep." Miley's dad understood where Aunt Dolly was going with this. "She said she was already datin' somebody else."

"And do you remember what I told ya?"

"Yep. You said, 'Next time you're gonna ask a girl out, don't wash your truck, wash your hair.'"

Aunt Dolly smiled. "I meant *after* that," she said.

"Yep. You said the only way you're out of the game is if you take yourself out of the game," he said.

Miley apparently saw where they were

going with this as well. "Guys, I know what you're doing. But let's face it: I waited too long and I blew it. Game over," she said.

"Robby, is this the same girl who came to me and said, 'I wanna be a singer,' and I said, 'Sweet pea, the chances of that happening are one in a million,' and she said, 'I wanna be that one'? Where is that girl?" Aunt Dolly asked.

Miley had to hand it to Aunt Dolly. "She's right here."

"Well, if you hadn't taken that risk, you never would've become Hannah Montana, now would ya?" Aunt Dolly asked, her voice rising with her pep talk. Aunt Dolly and Miley's dad sat down on either side of Miley.

"No," Miley grudgingly admitted.

"So . . ." Mr. Stewart waited for this all to

sink in so Miley would snap out of her funk.

"So if I want something bad enough, I gotta get off my butt and fight for it," she said with a slight lift in her voice.

"Well, that's right. It reminds me of a song by my favorite teen pop star." Dolly started to sing one of Hannah's songs. Mr. Stewart felt the need to join in, too. Miley started to laugh at them but couldn't resist joining in. They all high-fived after the big finish. Then Aunt Dolly, sitting close to Mr. Stewart, sniffed his arm suspiciously.

"Have you been using my citrus fizzy balls?" she asked him.

"No, ma'am. But I did use your apricot scrub." Then he walked away from her with a proud strut.

* * *

The next day, Miley was well on her way to recovering as she lay on a deck chair in a spa robe next to Aunt Dolly. Their faces were smeared with an avocado facial mask, and cucumber slices covered their eyes. Miley removed her cucumbers to talk to Dolly. "You know, Aunt Dolly, I kinda modeled Hannah Montana's look after you." Aunt Dolly, who was lying there with the bowl of avocado concoction, was excited.

"Really? I *thought* I was missing a wig!" she said, laughing.

Then another voiced chimed in. "Don't make me smile. I'm cracking." It was Mr. Stewart. He and Jackson were there in full spa regalia, too! Jackson took a chip from the bowl beside him, scraped some of his mask off with it, then shoved it in his mouth.

"You know, this avocado mask tastes ten times better than the mango scrub," he shared.

"You know, Rufus ate a whole bowl of that mango scrub once," Dolly replied. "For a week, that dog smelled like a tropical breeze coming and going!"

PART TWO

Chapter One

Hannah was in the middle of a concert, singing her heart out. This particular number was performed in polka-dot pajamas, and Hannah, along with her backup singers, was pretending to be at a slumber party, having a playful pillow fight. Feathers were flying all over the place. After the song ended, she dashed off-stage and found Lilly there, dressed as Lola in a short purple wig and a pearl choker.

"So, what'd you think?" Miley asked her best friend.

Lilly, being Lilly, focused on Miley's clothes and not her performance. "Those pajamas are soooooo cute."

Miley glared at her friend. "I was talking about the song."

"Oh, love that, too. But I can't wear it." She pointed to Miley with a smirk. "When we're at the mall tomorrow, I wanna get something cool to wear."

Miley had forgotten that they had plans to go shopping tomorrow. Now something had come up and she couldn't make it. "Oh, I forgot. Publicity thing. What about Saturday?"

"Saturday, Saturday . . . can't. Laker game with my dad. How about Sunday?" Lilly offered.

"Yes, I think I—" Miley tried to think

about whether or not she could do Sunday, but a wardrobe assistant pulled her into the dressing room to change outfits for the next part of the show. As she headed back onstage, she finished the thought. "—can't. Costume fitting Sunday morning. What about Sunday afternoon?"

"Ah, nope," Lilly replied. "Three o'clock dinner with my grandparents. I love 'em, but they smell like oat—" Lilly was cut off by the cheers of the crowd. Hannah was back onstage, and their conversation was officially over. After a long wait through Hannah's next song, Lilly finally got to finish her sentence "—meal," she said as Miley rushed off the stage once again, the crowd still roaring with cheers.

"Mmmm," Miley said. She was right there with Lilly the whole time. "I love the smell of oatmeal."

"Not when it's mixed with mouthwash and my grandmother's B.O.," she said, rolling her eyes and waving at her armpits. She paused for a minute and thought about something. "This is crazy," she said.

"What?" Miley asked.

"We haven't had any Miley/Lilly time in, like, forever." It was true. Between Miley's life as Hannah and all that entailed, and Lilly's busy but more run-of-the-mill life, they hadn't seen much of each other at all.

"I know," Miley said a little sadly. "I miss it, too."

"Then how about Tuesday after school?" Lilly suggested.

"Oh, sounds perfect . . ." Miley started to say, but yet again, she forgot she had plans. "But, I'm trying out for the cheer—" she was pulled back into the dressing room . . . again! Another few minutes passed, and

Part One

Miley was just about to kiss Jake in her daydream when she was interrupted by a buzzing sound.

"You were dreaming about Jake, weren't you?" Lilly asked.

"No, I wasn't. Why would I do that? I am so over him," Miley stated firmly.

"Why can't we do a song about whales—happy, independent girl whales?" Miley said.

"You okay, darlin'?" Mr. Stewart asked. His daughter just didn't seem like herself lately.

"Oliver, you took the wrong camera! Give it back!" Miley demanded.

"I've got to figure out something, Lilly," Miley said. "Jake's probably laughing at that tape right now."

"Let's focus on the plan. We grab the tape and we're outta here," instructed Miley.

Part Two

"Yes, I think I—can't. Costume fitting Sunday morning.
What about Sunday afternoon?" Miley asked.

"Cheerleading?" Lilly said. "Give me an N!
Give me an O!"

Lilly suprised everyone at cheerleading tryouts with an amazing series of tumbles and flips!

"I just did all my skateboarding stunts without my skateboard!" Lilly exclaimed.

From inside the giant pirate head, Miley had only one thing to say: *"Arrgggh!"*

"I am so glad you talked me into this," Lilly said. "It's a blast!"

"I did this cheerleading thing to be with Lilly. And now she's a cheerleader and I'm a lame pirate," said Miley.

"When I'm onstage performing, I look to the wings and you're always right there cheering me on," Miley said to Lilly.

Miley was pushed back out of the dressing room wearing a new top. She finished her sentence. " —leading squad. Oh, hey, why don't you try out with me?"

"Cheerleading? Give me an N! Give me an O! What's that spell? No." Lilly and cheerleading didn't exactly mix.

"Yeah, *no* time together. C'mon." She really wanted Lilly to try out with her. She did a cheer. "You can get this, we won't regret this, we'll be together, best friends forever!"

Lilly cheered back. "When you cheer this way, I have to say, 'Okay, I know you must be right.'" She noticed that their cheering had moved them onstage, in front of Hannah's whole screaming audience. She continued, "But now I have stage fright." Her talking had slowed down, and she was in shock.

Miley helped her friend along, "Say good

night, Lola," she directed her friend, holding her hand and waving it for her.

Lilly looked a little tentative, but she turned to the crowd and said nervously, "Good night, Lola!"

The next day, things were decidedly less glamorous at the Stewart home. Mr. Stewart was plunging the kitchen sink when Jackson walked in. "Hey, Dad, is the sink still clogged?"

As usual, Jackson was a master of the obvious. "No, son, I unclogged the sink hours ago, now I'm just working on my triceps." Jackson's father was obviously a little irritated.

"Well, here, let me help," Jackson suggested.

Mr. Stewart was taken aback. This wasn't exactly like his son. "Really?"

"Sure," he said enthusiastically. He walked over to his dad and adjusted his father's wrists. "If you lean into it like this, you'll get your deltoids, too."

Mr. Stewart should have known. "Maybe I'll just bench-press you out the window."

Jackson really didn't get it. "Are you working on your pecs or your delts? Make up your mind!"

"Oh, the heck with this. I'm already late for a meeting. I'm just gonna call the plumber." He headed for the phone, shaking his head in disgust. "I can't believe it, drain's already clogged, and now I'm gonna throw eighty dollars an hour down it." This little tidbit got Jackson's attention.

"Plumbers make eighty dollars an hour?" he asked. "I'll do it for fifty."

Mr. Stewart actually seemed interested

in this proposition. "You know what? I'm so late I'm gonna take you up on that little deal."

"Wait a minute, if I woulda known you were gonna cave that fast, I would've asked for, like, sixty," Jackson joked.

"And I was willing to give you seventy-five. Oh!" Mr. Stewart almost always got the last word where Jackson was concerned. He rushed out then, leaving Jackson to his task.

"All right, here we go!" he started plunging the drain with gusto, then stopped suddenly. "Wait a minute. If I'm gonna be a plumber, I'm gonna do this right." He stepped back, tugged at his jeans to lower them, and bent over again. "Oh, yeah. Ooh, that breeze feels nice." As he plunged away, he said, "Quickest fifty bucks I'll ever make." He flipped on the garbage disposal to test his work. The noises it made didn't sound promising. There was grinding and gargling and then silence. For a moment, Jackson thought he was in the clear. Then, there was a volcanic explosion that spewed the lavalike remnants of whatever had clogged the drain in the first place right in his face. He came up for air with a horribly sour expression on his now slimy face. "Oh, man," he groaned. "I hated that broccoli casserole the first time." Maybe that fifty bucks wasn't going to come so easily after all, he realized.

Chapter Two

Later that day, Miley and Lilly were practicing their cheers. They had a lot of work to do if they were both going to make the cheerleading squad. Dressed in sweats, Lilly sat and watched as Miley demonstrated a cheer for her. Wagging her pompoms, she shouted, "We've got pride!" Shake, shake, shake. "On our side!" Shake, shake, shake. "You know it, we show it! We've got pride!" she ended gleefully, with a giant flourish and a quick jump in the air. "Okay," she said to Lilly. "So, that's the pride cheer, with optional herkie. Any questions?"

"A couple. First, what the heckie is a herkie? And second," Lilly acted serious all of a sudden, "if one of these is a pom-pom, does that mean two of them are pom-pom-pom-poms? These are the questions that haunt me."

Miley wasn't amused. She really wanted Lilly to make the squad. "Show me what you got. Go ahead."

Lilly obliged her friend by doing the cheer with her own improvised dance moves that looked nothing like the ones Miley had just taught her. "Go team. Throw the ball. Go team . . ." She paused to think, and then, "To the mall!" She was obviously very pleased with herself. After all, who wouldn't want to go to the mall after the game? Lilly would move into the mall permanently if she could.

Miley was getting more and more exasperated. "Lilly, we're doing this to spend time together. That's not gonna happen if I'm on the team and you're not. Okay, so just watch me." She did some moves, looking like a polished cheerleader. Lilly tried to follow. "And, one-two-three-four. Move and squat, arms up and jump. Twirl, clap, arms up and jump. Okay, now you try."

Lilly went for it. As she did her cheer, Jackson and Mr. Stewart walked in. Jackson tried some of Lilly's moves right along with her. But the moves didn't turn out right, especially the twirling. "Move and squat and arms and jump and clap and . . . arms and . . . twirl, and twirling. Ah! How's that?" She had fallen over the back of the armchair in the living room and was facedown with her legs in the air.

"Now, why is it when I ended up on the couch like that you grounded me for a week?" Jackson asked his dad.

"'Cause you jumped all the way from the piano," Mr. Stewart explained.

"Sixteen feet—a new personal best, baby!" Jackson said.

Meanwhile, Lilly was still lying there. Miley walked over to her. "So I'm guessing you're going to be the only cheerleader there with pom-poms and a helmet."

"Ah, help," Lilly insisted. The girls promptly adjourned their practice and headed over to tryouts. Miley was going to have to pray for a miracle if she and Lilly were going to spend any time together. She crossed her fingers the whole way there.

* * *

After the girls left for tryouts, Jackson got back to work on the clogged sink. He just had to get that fifty bucks. He was up on the countertop hunched over the sink when Miley's friend Oliver walked in.

"Hey, Jackson. Where's Miley?" Oliver asked, looking at Jackson like he was a little crazy.

"Don't know," Jackson replied.

"When's she gonna be back?" Oliver asked. He was hoping for a little information here.

"Don't care," Jackson said.

"Will you tell her I dropped by?" Oliver asked. What was it going to take to get this guy to give Miley a message?

"Don't count on it," Jackson said. And then, with pride, "There, I'm through." But Oliver noticed something Jackson did not. He bent over to take a look under the cabinet. The snake that Jackson had run down the drain hadn't unclogged it at all. It had broken through the drainpipe and popped out entirely. He thought he'd better mention it to Jackson.

"Uh, Jackson?" he said, but Jackson was too busy being proud of himself to pay attention to Oliver.

"Uh, not right now, kid. I'm about to hit pay dirt," he said. Then he turned the water on, assuming it would run free and clear and that the fifty bucks would be his, all his. Instead, the water came shooting out of the broken pipe under the cabinet where Oliver happened to have his head buried. The thrust of the water was so great, it pushed Oliver back and sent him flying to the other side of the room!

"Jackson, turn it off! Jackson!" he yelled.

"Why does this always happen to me?" Jackson said as he took in the chaos that had occurred, thanks to his amateur plumbing skills.

"I was kinda thinkin' the same thing," Oliver lamented.

Later that day, Miley and Lilly were at school awaiting their turn to try out. They watched as Amber, cheering her heart out, clumsily fell to the ground. She cheered anyway, pom-poms flailing on the floor. It was a sight to behold, for sure. "Dominate the floor. Pirates make that score! Give it all you got! Pirates make that shot! Ow! I can't believe I broke a nail! Anyway," Amber went for a big finish, still lying there, "Yaaaaaay, team!" Amber teetered to her feet then, trying to save her image.

Coach Lewis, a former cheerleader

herself, was a perky observer. Sitting beside a giant bin filled with pom-poms and other cheerleading props, she was almost at a loss for words. "Ah, Amber . . . that was a wonderful effort. Every time you fell, you got right back up again." Then she paused and said, "Even when I begged you to stay down." Amber shrugged and limped over to her friend Ashley. Coach Lewis, ever the cheerleader, directed everyone to clap in support. "Everyone give it up for the effort." The weak applause died down pretty quickly. "Okay, moving on." Coach Lewis checked her clipboard to see who was next. Meanwhile, Ashley tried to offer her friend some encouraging words, albeit at the expense of Coach Lewis.

"She doesn't like you 'cause you're too pretty and you threaten her," she assured Amber.

"Story of my life!" Amber agreed as they walked out of the gym.

Coach Lewis then called on Miley. "Okay, Stewart. Show me your stuff!" Miley was a little anxious, but she felt pretty confident, too. She and Lilly gave each other a thumbs-up as Miley hopped to her feet and jogged to the middle of the gym floor. She took a short moment to breathe and psyche herself up, then she started her clap cheer. "They've got our ball." *Clap-clap*. "We want it back." *Clap-clap*. "They've got our ball." *Clap-clap*. "We want it back." *Clap-clap*. "They've got our ball—" but Coach Lewis interrupted her before she could finish.

"You want it back. Clap-clap. I get it. What else you got?" she challenged. Miley was a little thrown. She had been so sure of herself, and now the coach was questioning her. She recovered with another one.

"Oh, I've got a good one." She started a new cheer. "And slide and slide and do the butterfly! And dip and dip and shake my little hips, I want you and you to cheer it with me, too!" Coach Lewis seemed very pleased with this new cheer, and she led the girls in applause for Miley.

"Oh! Way to go, baby. When I asked you to bring it, you brought it. Now take it over there," she said to Miley, who was pleased as punch. She was beaming as she walked back to where she was sitting before her tryout. Next up was Lilly. "Lilly Truscott . . ." she bellowed in a game-show-host voice. "Come on down! You're the next contestant on 'The Coach Is Right!'" At first, no one seemed to understand that they were supposed to laugh at this bit, and it was silent in the room. Then, they all forced themselves to laugh, suddenly realizing that this was what the coach was expecting. She blew her whistle for their fake laughs to stop. "Okay, Truscott," she shouted to Lilly, "you're the last one. The next minute of my life is yours. Don't waste it."

Lilly shot a nervous look at Miley, who offered her a nod of encouragement. Lilly jogged over to the tryout area and started the cheer Miley had taught her; it was the same cheer Amber had ruined earlier. Lilly was pretty stiff. "Dominate the floor. Pirates raise that score! Give it a shot!— sorry, I mean—give it all you got! Pirates take that—make that—shot! Yay!" She tried to finish big but could tell it was a less than impressive tryout. When Lilly looked over at Miley, she could tell that her friend's thumbs-up was forced.

"Well, wasn't that something?" Coach Lewis tried to be her perky, encouraging self, too, but Lilly could see through it.

Lilly had a thought. She didn't want this audition to be over. She knew what it meant for her and Miley. "Uh, can I try something a little different?"

Coach Lewis eagerly agreed. "Yeah. Something different would be good." But Miley was a wreck. She turned to the girl sitting next to her and made a distressed face.

"Oh, no, I can't watch this. I only taught her one cheer." But Lilly started anyway. She seemed to know what she was doing. She clapped herself a beat and then started a cheer with some really amazing dance moves. "You might be good at football. You might be good at track. But when it comes to basketball, you might as well step back!

Come on, step back. Uh-huh. Uh-huh. Uh-huh." Then she did a very complicated, very cool jump-and-slide move. This didn't look a thing like the classic cheer moves Miley had taught her. Then, as Lilly geared up for a major gymnastics sequence, Miley had to cover her eyes. But there was no need. Lilly took a running start and completed an unbelievable series of tumbles and flips, the likes of which Miley had never seen. The whole room exploded with applause. Miley and Coach Lewis both ran up to Lilly at the same time. "Wow! Where did that come from?" Miley asked.

"I just did all my skateboarding stunts without my skateboard!" Lilly said, a little out of breath.

"Well, you know what? Put your skateboard away and grab a uniform. You're on the squad!" Coach Lewis cheered. Miley and Lilly jumped up and down, squealing with excitement. Coach Lewis turned to Miley next. "And Stewart, I love your enthusiasm. It is part of what makes you perfect for a position of great responsibility on this squad." Then, she said a singsongy voice, "And I think you know what I'm talking about."

Miley was sure she did know what Coach was talking about. She replied in the same singsongy voice, "I think I do." She looked at Lilly, "She's gonna make me head cheerleader."

But Coach Lewis had a different notion. "Congratulations to our new mascot!"

Miley seemed to have missed what she said, because she started to respond, "Yes!" before she realized what had just happened. "Mas-what?!" Coach Lewis reached into that big box of pom-poms and props and, much to Miley's horror, pulled out a giant pirate head and put it on Miley.

"Everyone say hello to Pirate Pete!" Coach Lewis instructed the group.

From inside the giant pirate head, Miley had only one thing to say: "Arrrgggh."

Chapter Three

The next day, the first cheerleading practice had begun, and Lilly and all the other cheerleaders were busy practicing their moves. In unison, they shouted, "We're number one, not number two. And we're gonna beat the 'whoops' out of you!" Meanwhile, Oliver, who was in charge of the sound board, spoke into the mic, and his voice echoed over the loud-speaker.

"Testing, testing. 5-5-5-0-1-2-1, 5-5-5-0-1-2-1. That's my number, ladies. The lucky tenth caller gets a date with . . . *moi*." Almost the second he finished talking, his cell phone rang. He picked it up with a suave look on his face. "Hello, lucky tenth caller."

"Knock it off, Oken!" Coach Lewis yelled into his ear.

"Sorry, Coach," Oliver said.

Then, in rare form, Miley pedaled her way into the gym. Her costume was outrageous. She was in a velvet pantalooned pirate suit, complete with a potbelly, a fake sword, a gold tooth, a rubber hook for a hand, and a fake stuffed parrot attached to her shoulder. And, to add insult to injury, she was a riding a tricycle—a tricycle!—with a skull-and-crossbones flag attached to it. "Arrrgh!" she shouted as convincingly as she could, ringing her tricycle bell. "I'm a pirate! Why am I riding a tricycle?" She rode in a circle around Coach Lewis, hoping for a good answer.

"This is not a tricycle, it's your pirate ship. Own it! Sell it! Make the crowd believe it!"

Miley rode off, muttering, "*I* don't even believe it," as the cheerleaders cheered, "Pirates make that score! Give it all you got! Pirates make that shot! Whew!"

Coach Lewis was thrilled. "Perfect! Fantastic! You girls are the best. There's not a girl in this school who doesn't wish she were you." Miley rang her tricycle bell to remind everyone that she was there. Coach Lewis acknowledged her dismissively. "Oh, hi, Stewart."

"Coach, I put this on my head, and it smells like a litter box," Miley complained.

"Don't worry, I think I've got something that might help," Coach Lewis replied as she went into her bag.

"Oh, man. There's gum stuck in here," Miley groaned. Coach Lewis walked over and showed her an array of air fresheners.

"Air fresheners!" the coach said with great enthusiasm. "Do you want to smell like a pine forest, a tropical breeze, or a brand-new car?"

Miley was mortified. "I wanna smell like a cheerleader," she said sadly.

"They don't make that scent. Now get back out there and show me a little less Miley and a lot more pedaling pirate. Arrrgh!" Coach Lewis urged before walking away from her.

Miley put her pirate head back on as Lilly approached with a bounce in her step.

"I am so glad you talked me into this. It's a blast," Lilly said.

"Oh, yeah! You should see it from in here," Miley said sarcastically. But Lilly was oblivious to Miley's pain.

"And the best part is, we're back to having Miley/Lilly time," Lilly said, smiling. A whistle blew then, which was Lilly's cue. "Gotta go," she said, just before she hurried away. Miley tried to leave, too, but her new wheels got the best of her. Just as she started to pedal off, she made a sharp turn that tipped her tricycle on its side, wheels spinning. She lay there like a turtle on its back, struggling to get up. To make matters even worse, Amber, Ashley, and another girl walked by at that exact moment.

"I know you feel bad about not making the squad," Amber said to the girl. "But look . . . arrgh!" She pointed to Miley—or what had become of Miley—and they all started laughing.

"See?" Ashley said as she and the other girls walked away. "I told you it would make you feel better."

"Oh, yeah, that's right, you run from Pirate Pete!" cried Miley. "If this thing had a plank, you'd be walkin' it!"

In her hurry to escape cheerleading practice, Miley had left her pirate head behind. Oliver, who had stayed a while longer so he could continue to annoy the girls and Coach Lewis, found the head and took it over to the Stewart house. There, he found Jackson pretty much where he had left him—at the kitchen sink. He dropped the pirate head on the couch and went over to Jackson, who was cleaning up his "plumbing tools."

"Hey, Jackson. Miley left her head at practice. You get it? Her head."

"Don't know," Jackson said.

"But I didn't ask—" Oliver said, confused.

"Don't care." This was starting to sound familiar to Oliver.

"Will you stop?" Oliver pleaded with Jackson.

"Don't count on it. Hey, check this out," Jackson said.

"One sec." Oliver wasn't about to get into the same situation he had been in earlier. He dove behind the kitchen island and poked his head up to have a look at Jackson's handiwork. "Ready," he indicated.

"Man, it was a little water and some unidentifiable sludge," Jackson said, referring to Oliver's earlier trauma. "Get a tetanus shot and buck up, little camper."

Then he turned the water on, and they both looked around the room, checking for leaks. There didn't seem to be any. "Ah, check it out! It's perfect!" Jackson shouted.

Oliver was skeptical but impressed. "How'd you do it?"

"I have absolutely no idea. I did know I had to work fast, though. Went under the house, it was dark, I got bit by spiders. Man, I wouldn't be surprised if I wake up tomorrow with super spidey powers." Then, to prove his skills even further, he grabbed some open cartons of leftover Chinese food, tossed the contents down the drain, and turned on the garbage disposal. "Hey, check this out," he said as they listened to the hum of the disposal in action. "That, sir, was the sweet and sour sound of fifty dollars going in my pocket."

But he spoke too soon. "Jackson!" his

father yelled from upstairs. Something was definitely wrong. Maybe there weren't any leaks *downstairs*, but what about upstairs?

"What's *that* sound?" Oliver asked.

Somehow, the Chinese food Jackson had dumped into the kitchen sink *downstairs*, had made its way through the pipes and onto Mr. Stewart, who was taking a shower in the *upstairs* bathroom! "Jackson!!!" he yelled again.

Downstairs, Jackson hoped those spidey skills had taken effect by now. "Man, I gotta get outta here!" He tried to shoot some webs out of his right wrist and then his left. He even did the sound effects. Needless to say, nothing worked. "Dang it!" he shouted desperately.

Jackson waited nervously for his father to descend the stairs. Finally, Mr. Stewart came down, still toweling his wet hair. He walked over to the sink where Jackson was standing.

"I know that it looks like I messed up," said Jackson. "But technically, the job was to unclog the sink, and the sink's unclogged. Now, I do take personal checks, but I prefer cash."

"And I prefer not to shower in moo shu pork. Now lunch is on me," Mr. Stewart said, as he picked something out of his hair and put it on Jackson. "And now it's on you."

Jackson stormed away from his father in frustration. As he stomped up the stairs, Miley entered through the front door. Immediately, she saw the pirate head sitting on the couch. She rolled her eyes. "Oh, no, it's following me," she groaned.

"Hey, Mile. How's it goin'?" her dad asked cheerfully.

"I feel like I've been dumped on all day,"

Miley said, having no idea how true that also was for her dad.

"Yeah, I know the feeling," he said.

Miley decided to spill the whole saga to her father. She had to let it out to someone. "I did this cheerleading thing to be with Lilly. And now she's a cheerleader and I'm a lame pirate! And yes, I'm talkin' to you, stinky," she said to her smelly pirate head, holding it up angrily.

Mr. Stewart sniffed the pirate. "Whoa. That's a relief. I thought it was me." He took the head from Miley and set it aside.

Miley was very upset. "I mean, I don't know what to do. I'm not having any fun. I just wish I could quit," she said.

"Well, then, why don't you?" Mr. Stewart suggested.

"What?" she asked. She hadn't even considered this option.

"I don't know any friendship that's worth wearing a smelly old pirate head for," Mr. Stewart said.

Miley clearly found this appalling. "How can you say that? She's my best friend. She's more important to me than . . ." She paused for moment, realizing that her dad had tricked her. "Wait a minute. Did you do that on purpose?" she asked.

Miley's father smiled. "Did what?"

"Got all Jedi mind-tricky on me again," she said. "Thanks, Dad. I'm gonna go take a shower."

Mr. Stewart felt he'd better warn Miley about the shower situation, rather than add to her terrible day. "Uh, unless you are in the mood for a moo-shooey shampooey, I wouldn't do that," he said.

Chapter Four

The next day, the stands were full for the Pirates' basketball game, and halftime was approaching. When the buzzer sounded, the players exited to the locker room, and Oliver announced the score. "And your score at halftime—the Fillmore Flamingos, fifty-eight, and your Seaview Pirates . . . less than that. Waaaaay less than that." He pushed one of his sound-effects buttons and the sound of a toilet flushing blared through the loudspeaker. "But let's not think about that; let's think about your lovely Seaview Pi-rettes!" Before signing off for the halftime routine, he quickly restated his phone number for anyone interested. "That's 555-0121."

The music started to pump, and Coach Lewis huddled with the girls. "Go, go! Okay, girls."

Oliver continued with his halftime show narration, announcing the arrival of the team mascot. "What's that I hear? Uh-oh! Cannon fire? It's Pirate Pete!" Miley had psyched herself up for this all day. She just kept remembering what her dad had said about her friendship with Lilly. What she was about to do—this embarrassing, ridiculous thing she was about to do—was for friendship. She rode into the gym on her tricycle, making a perfect circle—

without tipping over — in front of the crowd in the stands. She waved her sword victoriously and rallied the crowd.

"Arrgghh! Arrgghh! Let's chop up them flamingos and feed 'em to the sharks!" She came to a full stop in front of the stands. "Avast, ye landlubbers! Shiver me timbers!"

Her act was falling short, though. From the stands, someone yelled out, "Shiver your timbers over there! I can't see the cheerleaders!" Miley tried to move out of the way.

"Oh, sorry. I mean . . ." she had been speaking in her Miley voice. She quickly changed to her pirate voice. ". . . sorry, matey. Back it up! Whoa!" Only she backed up a little too much and a little too fast. She backed right into Amber and Ashley and their popcorn, which went flying.

"You're paying for that popcorn, you fat-headed freak!" Amber yelled.

Ashley joined her friend in making Miley feel terrible. "Shove off, matey!" she said, pushing Miley's tricycle. Miley, meanwhile, could not steady herself and backed right into Oliver who was, of course, holding a soda, which, of course, tipped over directly onto the sound board. The scene just kept getting worse. Sparks were flying, and then the sound board shorted out with a giant puff of smoke.

"No! Not my sound board!" Oliver shouted, desperately pressing buttons trying to salvage his precious piece of equipment. The "charge" music started but only for a moment. It petered out to a pathetic whine, then stopped entirely. The board was a goner.

"Sorry, Oliver!" Miley was a wreck. She

couldn't take another minute of this. She started to take off her pirate head, but Coach Lewis wouldn't have it.

"What are you doing? A mascot never takes off her head! It ruins the illusion!" she said dramatically.

"What illusion?" begged Miley. "I'm a pirate on a pink tricycle!"

"Look," Coach Lewis said, adjusting Miley's fake head so that she could see better, "just stay on the sidelines and watch the pretty cheerleaders." She pointed Miley in the direction of the bleachers, and Miley made her way there, trying to stay low so as not to obscure anyone's view. But the other team's mascot, the Fillmore Flamingo, had other plans. The big bird snuck up behind her and tapped her on the shoulder with his beak. Miley, at her wit's end, turned around as the bird assumed a fighting stance à la the Karate Kid.

"Take a hike, pinky. I'm not in the mood," Miley insisted. But the flamingo started to peck at her and wave his wings. She pushed him away. He pushed back. This was a time-honored tradition, two mascots fake-fighting each other, but Miley, being new to the mascot trade, didn't know this. "I said, back off!" she shouted. They started to shove each other harder, and the crowd got involved, even as the cheerleaders continued with their routine on the court. As Lilly climbed to the top of the cheerleader pyramid, the mascot fight hit fever pitch, and Miley and her pink, feathery counterpart fell to the ground, rolling across the gym floor entwined in each other's costumes. Like a bowling ball headed for a strike, the mascot mess rolled toward the pyramid, hit the bottom row, and knocked it over, sending all the cheerleaders, including Lilly, tumbling to the ground.

Miley didn't even seem to care. She was going to finish this fight. "Bring it on, birdie! Why, you little—! Hey! Stop it! Ow! Ouch! Ouch! Ouch! Oh, I'm gonna get you for that. Hey, no pecking! How do you think I got this eye patch?" Coach Lewis stepped in and pulled the mascots apart. She escorted Miley out of the gym so she could have a little chat with her. In the hallway, Miley took off her pirate head at long last and held it in her hands. She looked at Coach Lewis, ashamed. "I'm sorry, coach, I was just trying to be the best mascot I could be."

"And I think you were," the Coach said, half-smiling. "That's what's so sad."

"But, I'll be better next time," Miley said.

Then she saw how her coach was looking at her. "There won't be a next time, will there?"

"Listen, sweetie, some people just aren't meant to perform in front of crowds. What I'm trying to say is, Beyoncé you're not. Turn in your head. But have it dry-cleaned first." She headed back into the gym, leaving Miley behind.

Then, Lilly came out to see Miley. "Hey, what happened?" she asked.

"I've been fired. I'm sorry, Lilly, I really wanted this to work out. But we can find something else we can do together. Come on," she said, assuming Lilly would just walk away from the squad.

"What do you mean, 'come on'? I have to go back out and cheer," she told Miley.

"Why would you go back out if I'm not there?" Miley asked, thoroughly confused.

"Because . . . well, I like it," Lilly admitted, a little embarrassed.

"But you only did this so we could be together," Miley said. How could this be?

"That's before I saw how cute I looked in this uniform." It always came down to clothes with Lilly.

"So a uniform's more important than our friendship?" Miley accused.

"No, but—" The ref whistled from inside the gym. The second half was starting and Lilly had to get back inside. "Miley, can we not do this now?" She looked at the door to the gym. "I have a big herkie coming up!"

Miley was getting more and more upset. "You didn't even know what a herkie was until I taught you!" But Coach Lewis beckoned Lilly.

"Truscott!"

"Look, I gotta go," Lilly said sadly.

"Well, so do I!" They both headed off in opposite directions. Miley stopped for a minute and looked back at Lilly, who just kept walking. Miley started away again. Then Lilly stopped and turned around and saw Miley walking away from her. Neither one had seen the other turn around.

Back at the Stewart house, the plumbing disaster was finally being addressed by a professional. The plumber was there, bent over the sink with his underwear showing, in that classic plumber position Jackson had tried to imitate earlier. "Well, Mr. Stewart, you are one lucky man," the plumber said.

"Oh, I'd feel luckier if I were talking to your face," Mr. Stewart joked.

"Oops, sorry, was I showing again?" The plumber stood up then. "You get so used to the breeze, you can't even tell any-more."

Jackson remembered that feeling well. "I know what you mean," he said wistfully.

"Your main line was so rusted, you were one flush away from flooding the place. But the work this boy did held it all together until I got here." The plumber's words were shocking to both Mr. Stewart and Jackson.

"Now, wait a minute, are you talkin' 'bout my son, Jackson? This boy right here? My son?" Mr. Stewart asked incred-ulously.

"He didn't screw up," the plumber said emphatically. "He saved this place."

"This boy did?" Mr. Stewart asked once again.

"Yeah!" The plumber said, running out of ways to say it.

"Jackson?" Mr. Stewart was unwilling

to accept the fact that Jackson really could have helped the situation.

"Yes! Son, you've got the plumber's gift. My boy had it, but he decided to go to college. Kids, they'll break your heart," he said mournfully. He gathered his things and left, leaving Jackson and his father alone.

"Well, I guess someone owes someone an apology. And fifty bucks," Jackson said with great pride.

"You're right, Jackson. I never thought I'd ever say this, but, good job, son. I'm proud of ya." Mr. Stewart took some money out of his wallet and handed it to Jackson before heading upstairs.

"'Good job, son. Good job. Thanks, Jackson. You're welcome, Dad,'" Jackson play-acted. "Yeah, I could get used to this." He started singing and drumming on the counter. "'Cause I didn't screw up, I didn't screw up, I didn't screw up cha-cha, I didn't screw up!—" He moved his drumming to the refrigerator door, but a crash stopped his celebration. He slowly opened the door to find the shelves completely collapsed; the food inside started crashing to the floor.

"Jackson, what was that?!" Mr. Stewart yelled from upstairs. Jackson once again prayed that his spidey powers had kicked in. He tried to shoot webs out of each of his wrists . . . to no avail . . . again.

"Nothing! It's time for my spidey escape." He hopped up on the counter and squatted in front of the kitchen window, trying once again to shoot webs from his wrists. "Dang it, I gotta get these things fixed," he said and waited for Mr. Stewart to find him out.

Chapter Five

Miley had headed home after the basketball game fiasco to get changed into her Hannah gear for a big party she was invited to that night. As she was adjusting her wig in the living room, Lilly walked in. Or rather, Lilly limped in, still wearing her cheerleading outfit. She was visibly upset. "Okay, now I'm ready to talk!" she said to Miley.

Miley was sarcastically apologetic. "Well, now I can't. Hannah Montana has a backstage party at the Stones concert." She was a little concerned about Lilly's limp, however. "Why are you limping?"

"Because, thanks to you, I couldn't concentrate, and my herkie was jerky," Lilly said.

"Wow, that looks swollen. Do you want some ice?" Miley offered.

"Don't you be nice to me when I'm mad at you—and yes, wrapped in a towel," she added. Miley headed to the kitchen for ice and put some in a dish towel, as requested.

"Can you still cheer?" Miley asked curiously.

"It doesn't matter anyway. I'm gonna quit," she said flatly.

"What? You can't," Miley protested.

"What are you talking about? You're the one who told me I should!" Lilly shouted with tremendous exasperation in her voice.

"Well, I was being selfish. When I'm onstage performing, I look out to the wings, and you're always right there cheering me on. Well, I just want to do the same thing for you." She had thought about this the whole way home from the game. She had really been unfair to Lilly, and she felt terrible about it.

"Really?"

"Yeah," she said, putting the ice gently on Lilly's ankle. "But I can't do that if you quit."

"But if I don't quit, we'll never get any Miley/Lilly time together. And I mean, it's not like you can quit being Hannah Montana," she said. This was the truth. This was how the whole thing started in the first place.

"No," Miley agreed. "But sometimes I can." She took off her wig. "Like tonight."

Lilly was truly surprised. "What are you doing?"

"I'm about to limp to the mall with my friend, Lilly," Miley said, smiling.

"You're gonna give up the Rolling Stones concert for me?" Lilly asked. She couldn't believe it.

"Please, those guys'll still be touring when they're ninety," said Miley.

"I thought they *were* ninety," said Lilly. They both giggled at that and then exchanged a big hug.

Put your hands together for the next Hannah Montana book . . .

Nightmare on Hannah Street

Adapted by Laurie McElroy

Based on the series created by Michael Poryes and Rich Correll & Barry O'Brien

Based on the episode, "Torn Between Two Hannahs," Story by Valerie Ahern & Christian McLaughlin

Teleplay by Todd J. Greenwald

Miley Stewart, along with her best friends Lilly and Oliver, listened to her father play a new song. Mr. Stewart strummed his guitar and then launched into the lyrics. Miley joined in with her strong, clear voice, reading the lyrics her father had written.

When the song was over, Lilly and Oliver applauded wildly. Not only was it a terrific song, it was perfect for Hannah Montana.

Miley's best friends were the only two people in the world outside of her family who knew her secret.

When it came to secrets, this was a big one.

Miley Stewart led a double life. Most days she was just a regular seventh grader. But at night, she became pop-music sensation Hannah Montana. Hannah was the queen of the teen music world.

Miley loved being Hannah onstage, but offstage she was happy to take off her blond Hannah wig and pop-star clothes and go back to being Miley Stewart. She wanted people to like her for who she was and not because she was famous. That meant living like a regular girl and keeping her double life a secret.

Miley gave her father a high-five. She knew this new song would make Hannah more popular than ever. "Dad, that's awesome. That is the best song you've ever written. I can't wait to record it."

Then Miley remembered the last time her father wrote her a really great song. The song was the best. But the news that came along with it was the worst. "What's the bad news?" she asked.

"Bad news?" Lilly asked, confused. "What are you talking about? It's a great song."

"Thank you, Lilly," Mr. Stewart said. He turned to Miley. "I've always liked her," he said, nodding in Lilly's direction.

"Don't change the subject," Miley said seriously.

Mr. Stewart *did* have some news, but he wasn't telling—yet. Lilly and Oliver looked even more confused.

"Every time he has bad news he tries to soften it with a great song," Miley explained to her friends. She had a list of top-ten songs and the bad news that went along with them, and she could tell the list was about to get longer. She laid some of them out for Lilly and Oliver.

"'Best of Both Worlds'—I had to get braces. 'This Is the Life'—Jackson decided not to go to sleepaway camp. 'Pumpin' Up the Party'—my goldfish died."

Miley's goldfish triggered one of Oliver's memories. "When my goldfish died, my mom flushed it down the toilet," he said. "I'll never forget her comforting words—

'Get over it, Oliver, it's a stinking fish.'"

Lilly nodded knowingly. "That explains so much."

But Miley didn't want to hear about Oliver's fish. "Come on, Dad, just tell me. Trust me, I can handle it."

Mr. Stewart took a breath and then spit the words out. "Your cousin Luann is coming to visit," he said quickly. Then he turned to Lilly and Oliver and tried to change the subject. "Who wants pie?"

Luann? Miley stared at her father, completely stunned. That was the worst news ever. When she became Hannah Montana, Miley, her father, and her brother had left Tennessee and moved to California.

Miley loved her new friends and their beach house in Malibu, but sometimes she missed everyone in the big extended family they had left back home. Everyone except

Luann. The name Luann was so horrifying to her that Miley couldn't speak, couldn't move, couldn't scream.

"Miley?" Lilly asked

"Miley?" Mr. Stewart repeated, waving a hand in front of her face.

Miley didn't even blink. She was totally frozen.

Oliver didn't notice. "What kind of pie?" he asked, jumping to his feet and running to the kitchen.

"C'mon, Mile," Mr. Stewart said. "Don't forget that wonderful, wonderful song that I just wrote you, that you love so much." He picked up his guitar again and sang as he played.

Miley put her hand on the guitar strings, stopping him. She didn't want to hear the song right now—not when her father had just spit out the terrible news. "When does her broomstick land?" she asked through clenched teeth.

"Come on there, Mile. Don't start this again," Mr. Stewart said, heading toward the kitchen. "She's a good kid. Let's not forget who pulled you out of that well when you were just six."

"Let's not forget who pushed me in," Miley said, following him.

"Hey, that was an accident. Sometimes kids do stuff without thinking," Mr. Stewart said.

Miley shook her head. Luann had their parents totally fooled, but Miley knew the truth. Luann was bad news—really bad news.

Oliver had cut himself a huge slice of cherry pie and was eating it at the kitchen table. A fly buzzed around his head and landed on his slice. He slammed his hand down, missing the fly, but knocking his plate into his lap and getting pie all over himself. "Stupid fly," Oliver said, spreading cherry filling across his T-shirt.

Miley and Lilly looked on in disbelief as he picked up his fork and started eating again. But Mr. Stewart used Oliver's mess to make his point about accidents.

"I didn't plan that," he said. "But there you go."

"I can't believe this," Miley said. "Halloween is two days away, and you want me to share my bathroom with the Princess of Darkness? If she's coming, I'm sleeping at Lilly's." Miley turned on her heel and stormed toward the front door.

"Oh, come on, Mile," her father said, trying to reason with her. "You guys have both grown up. She's grown up. You've grown up. You're a lot alike."

Alike? Miley turned to her father, totally outraged. "How can you say that? I'm nothing like that horrible, ugly witch."

The doorbell rang. Miley opened the front door and found herself face to face with her hated cousin. Luann was in all her Tennessee finery—pigtails, a bright red shirt that looked like an overgrown bandanna, and a straw cowboy hat. People had been telling both girls for years that they looked alike, but Miley didn't see it. She glared at her cousin.

Luann blinked behind her glasses and flashed Miley a big grin. "Howdy, cuz!" she said.

Lightning flashed, followed by a crash of thunder. Evil is in the air, Miley thought.

Lilly's jaw dropped, and she was too stunned to close it again. Oliver's eyes popped. Luann and Miley looked like twins!

Luann ignored everyone's shock and confusion. "Eeeee doggies!" she declared. "This is one humdinger of a shack!"